Julie Andrews Edwards & Emma Walton Hamilton

Dumpy
saves Christmas

Illustrated by Tony Walton

Hyperion Books for Children/New York

WHOOOOSH! A gust of wind made the weather vane on the red barn roof spin merrily. The old rooster flapped his wings dizzily in an effort to keep his balance.

Everyone at Merryhill Farm was spinning that day, for it was
Christmas Eve—and there was *much* to do.

"Looks like we're in for some more snow," Pop-Up said to his
grandson Charlie as they hurried toward the barn. "We'll give
Dumpy a can of antifreeze so his radiator won't ice up."

They opened the barn doors, and Charlie gazed lovingly at the colorful little dump truck parked inside.

"Dumpy needs a blanket to keep his engine warm," he said.

Pop-Up grinned.

"Your mom thinks *we* need one when we're driving him. We fixed him up good as new — but he's still a little drafty!"

"I'll ask Santa Claus to bring him one when I make my list tonight!" said Charlie.

As they walked back to the farmhouse, Trusty the Mail Truck was pulling away from the front porch.

"**WOTTLE-WOTTLE-WOTTLE-WOT!**" Trusty wheezed. "Through hail and sleet and dead of night, your mail will reach you, come **WOT** might!"

"Not a moment too soon!" Pop-Up winked at Mrs. Barnes as they whisked the packages indoors.

"Merry Christmas!" Charlie waved as Trusty puffed and gasped his way down the drive.

The farmhouse was full of the sounds and smells of Christmas: logs crackling in the fireplace; carols jingling on the radio; spicy aromas of cinnamon, gingerbread, and clementines filling the air. Best of all—the tree itself, pine-scented and twinkling from head to toe.

After a delicious supper, the family settled in front of the fire to hang stockings while Charlie wrote to Santa Claus.

DEAR SANTA, he printed carefully.

His father attached the note to the mantel with a strong thumbtack, and Charlie hugged everyone good night.

"Merry Christmas, pal," Pop-Up said lovingly.

"Sweet dreams, noodle," said Farmer Barnes.

Mrs. Barnes tucked Charlie into his comfy bed and kissed his brow. "Go straight to sleep, peanut . . . Santa can't come while you're awake!"

Charlie squeezed his eyes shut, but his head was buzzing with questions. How did Santa reach all the children in one night? How did the sleigh hold so many presents?

Charlie opened one eye, but it was still dark. He decided to count trucks. There was Dumpy, of course, and Trundle the Tractor and Bee-Bee the Backhoe on the farm, Big Red the Fire Engine at the station, and Tommy the Tow Truck at the garage.

Charlie was just beginning to fall asleep when there was a large
THUMP! outside his window. He sat up.
SCREEECH! CLATTER, CLATTER, STOMP! JINGLE!
"DRAT!" said a voice. Charlie scrambled to the window and
gasped with amazement.

On the porch roof,
listing to one side and in danger
of falling off altogether, was a GREAT
BIG SLEIGH! Nine reindeer were skittering
to keep their balance on the icy shingles. A red-clad
figure was bending over, examining a badly damaged runner.

"Phooey! Fiddlesticks! BOTHER!"
Charlie cracked the window open and asked timidly,
"What happened?"

Startled, the red-clad figure popped up and spun around.

"Whoa! Ho, ho!" he said as he nearly fell backward. "Shouldn't you be asleep, young man?"

Charlie was speechless. He was face-to-face with Santa Claus.

"It's Rudolf's allergies." The jolly old man sighed. "His nose just isn't beaming tonight. We've had bumps and dings all across America, and now we've missed your chimney and my sleigh is busted." He scratched his beard. "What am I going to do? I still have *so* many presents to deliver!"

Charlie thought about how sad all the children would be if Santa never came.

"Could you use our dump truck?" he asked. "Dumpy can carry anything!"

"It's a little unorthodox. . . ." said Santa doubtfully.

"But the reindeer could pull him," Charlie offered. "Just like your sleigh."

". . . and the elves can fix the sleigh while we're gone!" Santa slapped his knee. "Ho, ho, it's brilliant! But we must hurry!"

Charlie tiptoed downstairs and raced to the barn.

"Wake up, Dumpy!" he whispered. "Santa needs you!"

Dumpy blinked sleepily.

"This is one fine truck you have here, Charles," said Santa. "Lucky that Rudolf chose *your* house to bump into!"

He attached the reindeer to Dumpy, and climbed up onto the cab roof. Grinning, he called down to Charlie, "Well, what are you waiting for? Hop in!"

"Me?" said Charlie.

"Jobs don't get more important than this. I'm usually halfway around Europe by now. . . . *Someone's* gotta steer this truck, or we'll never be finished by dawn!"

Santa draped a huge plaid blanket around Charlie's shoulders.
"It sparkles up there, but it sure gets chilly! Now, let's get started!"
Charlie scrambled aboard and turned the key in the ignition.
Dumpy's engine coughed and sprang to life. The reindeer strained
in their harness. Santa gave the command.
"ON, Dasher! ON, Donner! ON, Comet! ON, Blitzen!"
"ON, DUMPY!" yelled Charlie, and they soared into the night.

What a ride it was!

Heading east, they flew to London, and chimney-hopped their way across the city. They had a bird's-eye view of Big Ben just as the famous old clock was chiming midnight. **BONG! BONG!** "**TOOT! TOOT!**" Dumpy called back.

Despite his heavy load, Dumpy was
so exhilarated to be airborne that
by the time they reached Paris,
he insisted on flying around
the Eiffel Tower twice just
to enjoy the view.

They zoomed over the Swiss Alps, sparkling in the moonlight, dropping packages to every cozy chalet nestled in the snow.

But on the descent to Italy, poor Rudolf started sneezing again, and they narrowly missed bumping into the Leaning Tower of Pisa. "Easy, fella!" called Santa. "It's tilted enough as it is!"

On they sped to Greece. Charlie recognized the wondrous Acropolis from the pictures he'd seen in his geography books. Santa banked down for a closer look, and the ancient columns wobbled as Dumpy thundered between them and out the other side.

"I really shouldn't do that." Santa grinned. "But I can never resist!"

They headed south for Africa, and soared over the deserts, jungles, and pyramids . . . then —

WHOOSH! Up they went to the frosted domes of Moscow.

"The world is *so* beautiful!" said Charlie.

"All the more reason to take care of it," said Santa. He looked at his watch. "We're cutting it close. We should be in New Zealand by now."

"Does *everybody* celebrate Christmas?" Charlie asked.

"Not everybody . . ." the old man replied. "Some people celebrate Hanukkah, some Kwanza. Some celebrate different things at different times of the year. But everyone carries a message of love in their heart, no matter what their language or when they celebrate."

Soon they were flying over India's Taj Mahal. Dumpy's load of gifts had lightened considerably, but he was beginning to feel a little bleary from the urgent speed of their mission.

Rudolf's condition was worsening as he sneezed his way across China and Japan.

"Hang in there, old fella!" called Santa. "Vacation next week—you'll get your glow back!" But as the moon faded, Santa found it even harder to navigate.

"Australia's around here somewhere. . . . If *only* we had more light!"

"HEADLIGHTS!" Charlie cried, and flipped a switch on the dashboard. Dumpy careened across the outback like a blazing comet, narrowly missing several startled kangaroos and sleepy koala bears.

Moments later, they glimpsed the faintest lavender blush on the horizon.

"There's the dawn!" Santa pointed. "We're never going to make it, Chuck!"

And indeed, as they delivered packages across Hawaii, the islands were already glowing like amethysts on a jeweled necklace.

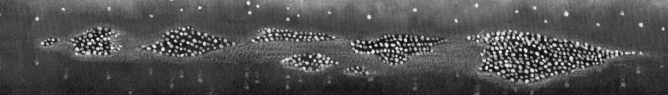

"Oh, *please*, Dumpy!" Charlie cried. "Think of all the children! Isn't there something more you can do?"

Dumpy was so frazzled that his engine was knocking, but he took a deep breath, hunched down, and with a shudder that rattled his frame, he BLASTED into overdrive.
"**BRROOOM! BRROOOM!**" he roared, and they rocketed up the East Coast.

"HOORAY!" cried Charlie.

"BRAVO!" yelled Santa. "A gold star for Dumpy!" And he plucked the last one out of the sky just as Apple Harbor's lighthouse came into view.

Over the schoolhouse they flew, past the post office, past Pharaoh's General Store, delivering their last gifts to the sleepy little village.

Soft snowflakes were falling as they touched down at Merryhill Farm. They unbuckled the reindeer from Dumpy's fender and tucked the world-weary little truck safely into the barn.

"Good job, Dumpy," Charlie whispered lovingly.

"This fine fella saved Christmas," said Santa, and he pinned the gold star on Dumpy's radiator cap. Dumpy sighed happily.

"As for you, Charlie," Santa said, "I hereby declare you an honorary elf!"

Charlie hugged him. "That was the best geography lesson I ever had!"

He ran to his bedroom and climbed into bed just as Santa's newly repaired sleigh soared past his window with a **WHOOSH!** and a **JINGLE!**

"Merry Christmas, pal!" Santa cried, his voice receding into the distance.

"Merry Christmas, pal! Merry Christmas!" Charlie felt a gentle hand on his shoulder. Pop-Up's face loomed above him. "Wait till you see! It's a white world this morning!"

"I had the most amazing dream. . . ." Charlie marveled.

"Tell me all about it," said Pop-Up. "But let's hurry! I'm itching to get at those presents!"

And what a lot there were—spilling from under the tree in all colors, shapes, and sizes. Mrs. Barnes got a fat new canary, and Farmer Barnes squeezed a happy tune from his new concertina.

Pop-Up did a little jig as he unwrapped a jolly red hat and a scarf to match.

The biggest box was for Charlie, and he gasped with delight at the shiny bright globe inside.

"Here's a present for Dumpy!" Pop-Up pulled one last package from under the tree. Charlie tugged at the ribbon and tissue paper, and was amazed to discover a fluffy plaid blanket—*exactly* like the one from Santa's sleigh.

"Let's take it to Dumpy right now!" he cried.

The entire family waded through the fresh snow, and as they opened the doors to the barn, Charlie hugged the blanket and said, "Won't Dumpy be surprised?"

But the surprise was all Charlie's. As the Christmas sun flooded in, he saw something on his beloved dump truck that took his breath away.

Sparkling and winking on Dumpy's radiator cap was a glorious gold star.

"How did *that* get there?" Mrs. Barnes asked.

Pop-Up scratched his beard. "Beats me," he replied.

Perhaps Charlie *hadn't* been dreaming, after all.

For Katherine, Anne, and Lisa with love and thanks

Printed in the United States of America
This book is set in 19-point Colwell.
The artwork for each picture was prepared using watercolor and colored pencil.

FIRST EDITION
1 3 5 7 9 10 8 6 4 2

Library of Congress Cataloging-in-Publication Data
Edwards, Julie, 1935–
Dumpy saves Christmas / Julie Andrews Edwards and Emma Walton Hamilton ;
illustrated by Tony Walton.—1st ed.
p.   cm.
Summary: When Santa's sleigh crashes at Merryhill Farm, Dumpy the dump truck
and his friend Charlie deliver presents around the world.
ISBN 0-7868-0743-1 (hc)
[1. Christmas—Fiction. 2. Santa Claus—Fiction. 3. Dump trucks—Fiction. 4. Trucks—Fiction.]
I. Hamilton, Emma Walton. II. Walton, Tony, ill. III. Title.

PZ7.E2562 Ds   2001
[E]—dc21   00-46170

Visit www.hyperionchildrensbooks.com